AT HOME

SAFETY

K. Carter

The Rourke Press, Inc.
Vero Beach, Florida 32964

PHOTO CREDITS
All photos © Emil Punter/Photovision

Library of Congress Cataloging-in-Publication Data

Carter, Kyle, 1949–
  At Home / Kyle Carter
    p. cm. — (Safety)
  Includes index
  ISBN 1-57103-080-8
  1. Safety education—Juvenile literature. 2. Children's acci-
dents—Prevention—Juvenile literature. [1. Dwellings—Safety mea-
sures. 2. Safety]
I. Title II. Series: Carter, Kyle. 1949-   Safety
HQ770.7.C37   1994
363.1'07'083—dc20   94–18133
                                              CIP
Printed in the USA   AC

TABLE OF CONTENTS

HOME SAFETY

You want your home to be a safe and secure place. It can be, but it can also be dangerous.

More than 20,000 Americans die in home accidents each year. Another 3,000,000 are seriously injured. That doesn't mean you should be afraid of your home or share a shell with a turtle. It does mean that you need to be alert to danger in the home.

By removing some of the causes of home accidents, you can help avoid having one!

REACHING HOME SAFELY

Home safety begins by reaching home safely. If you ride a school bus, stay quietly in your seat. Do not distract the bus driver. If you ride in a car to home, buckle your seat belt.

When you leave the bus or car, check to be sure the street is clear of traffic.

If you walk home, follow busy, well-lighted streets to your home. If you have to let yourself in, keep your house key in a safe place on you.

Keep your house key in a safe place

ELECTRICITY

Electricity and the home **appliances** it operates make our lives easier. If electricity is used carelessly, it can shock, burn and even kill you.

Electricity is attracted to water. Always dry your hands before touching an electric appliance, such as a radio, toaster or hairdryer.

Never use an electric appliance near a sink or a tub with water in it.

SLIPS AND TRIPS

You expect to fall now and then on ice. You can fall just as easily at home. As a matter of fact, falls kill more people than any other kind of accident!

You can avoid many household falls by walking instead of running. On stairways, hold onto the railing.

Be very careful when you step into or out of a tub or shower. Ask for **non-skid** mats in the tub.

Leave firearms in the house alone!

Whenever possible, walk home with friends

PICKING UP AND CLIMBING UP

Picking up helps prevent someone—perhaps you— from falling down.

Pick up shoes, rollerblades and other items that might later trip someone. Never pile books or toys on the stairs.

If you spill a liquid, clean it up. Wet floors are slippery floors.

If you need something that you can't reach, ask an adult for help. Never climb on chairs, cabinets, tables or boxes.

Climbing on furniture for hard-to-reach objects is dangerous

POISONS

Never taste, sniff, drink or eat anything that you don't recognize. Many homes adopt the rule that "if it's not in the refrigerator, it should not be opened."

Nearly every home has bottles, cans, tubes and other containers that hold dangerous materials. They are often such things as medicines, cleaning fluids, garden supplies and insect poisons. Any one of these products can be a deadly poison. Leave them alone!

*Leave medicine bottles and
other containers alone*

DON'T PLAY WITH FIRE

Only traffic accidents, falls and drownings cause more **accidental** deaths than fires. You can help keep your home fire-free by never playing with matches, lighters or any open flame. Be sure to keep loose clothing away from stoves, ovens and the fireplace.

Discuss with your family an escape plan in case of fire. Know the emergency number to call if you have a fire.

An emergency operator will help. You need to remember the emergency number, such as 9-1-1, in your area

TORNADO ALERT

Tornadoes are extremely dangerous, whirling winds. They sometimes develop during hard thunderstorms.

The safest place to be at home during a tornado is in the basement. If your home does not have a basement, stay on the lowest floor. Lie flat and pull a blanket over you. A blanket will help protect you from breaking glass.

A tornado destroyed this house

FIREARMS

Firearms, or guns, cause about 1,400 accidental deaths each year in the United States. Many of these deaths are in homes.

Guns should always be stored unloaded and locked away, but often they are not.

If you find a gun in your home or elsewhere, don't handle it. Treat any firearm as if it were just as dangerous as a huge rattlesnake. It is.

Glossary

accidental (ak suh DEN tul) — that which happens by chance

appliance (uh PLI entz) — any of several household devices, such as refrigerators, that operate by gas or electricity

firearms (FIRE armz) — guns

non-skid (NON-SKID) — a surface covering that is made to especially reduce the chance of someone slipping on that surface

tornado (tor NAY do) — a powerful, whirling windstorm that can cause severe damage

INDEX